The Big Ball

Story by Annette Smith

Illustrations by Chantal Stewart

Monkey said to Rabbit,

"Here comes the ball."

Look at Rabbit.

Monkey said to Little Teddy,

"Here comes the ball."

Look at Little Teddy.

Monkey said to Little Teddy,

"Here comes the ball."

"No, Monkey. **No!**" said Rabbit.

"The ball is too big."

"Here is a little ball,"

said Rabbit.

Monkey said to Little Teddy,

"Here comes the little ball."